THE CAT IN THE
Knows a Lot About That!

Walkin' in a Sticker Wonderland!

Based on a television script by Karen Moonah
Written by Michael Joosten
Illustrated by Christopher Moroney

A GOLDEN BOOK · NEW YORK

TM & copyright © by Dr. Seuss Enterprises, L.P. 2012. All rights reserved.
Published in the United States by Golden Books, an imprint of Random House Children's Books, a division of Random House, Inc., 1745 Broadway, New York, NY 10019.
Golden Books, A Golden Book, and the G colophon are registered trademarks of Random House, Inc. Based in part on *The Cat in the Hat Knows a Lot About Christmas!*
holiday special © CITH Productions, Inc. (a subsidiary of Portfolio Entertainment, Inc.), and Red Hat Animation, Ltd. (a subsidiary of Collingwood O'Hare Productions, Ltd.),
2010–2011. THE CAT IN THE HAT KNOWS A LOT ABOUT THAT! logo and word mark TM 2010 Dr. Seuss Enterprises, L.P., Portfolio Entertainment, Inc.,
and Collingwood O'Hare Productions, Ltd. All rights reserved. The PBS KIDS logo is a registered trademark of PBS. Both are used with permission. All rights reserved.
Broadcast in Canada by Treehouse™. Treehouse™ is a trademark of the Corus® Entertainment Inc. group of companies. All rights reserved.
Visit us on the Web!
randomhouse.com/kids   Seussville.com   pbskids.org/catinthehat   treehousetv.com
ISBN 978-0-307-93197-9   Printed in the United States of America   10 9 8 7 6 5 4 3 2 1

The Cat in the Hat is having a Christmas party!

The Cat has invited all his friends to celebrate the holiday.

Everyone joins in the candy-tastic candy-cane hunt.
Can you find all the candy canes?

Everyone hangs shiny decorations on the Christmas tree.

Now it's time to decorate the gingerbread house.

All the delicious cookies have been baked.
Draw a line from each cookie to its tasty match.

Everyone enjoys eating Christmas cookies.

Before they know it, it's time for everyone to make their way home for Christmas.

The first stop will be Ralph's home in . . . Freeze-Your-Knees Snowland!

Along the way, the Thinga-ma-jigger has engine trouble. The Cat in the Hat has to make an emergency landing in the African savanna.

Luckily, the Cat has friends who live in the Dizzle-Dazzle Desert:
Effia, Thimba, and Bisa.

The Thinga-ma-jigger needs water so it will cool down.
Help the Cat in the Hat and his friends find the watering hole.

ANSWER:

Connect the dots to see what animal is swimming in the watering hole.

The Thinga-ma-jigger has finally cooled down and is ready for takeoff.

On the way to Ralph's, the Cat and his friends decide to visit Christmas Island!

Daphne the Dolphin welcomes everyone!

Thing One and Thing Two are excited to make a giant sand castle on the beach.

Sally and Nick climb the palm trees to get coconuts.

Mervin the Crab leads a crab march on the beach.

The quick visit has been a lot of fun.

It's time to get Ralph back to his home.

It's cold in Freeze-Your-Knees Snowland, so time to bundle up.

Ralph introduces his parents to all his friends.

How many times can you find the word SNOW in the puzzle?
Look up, down, forward, backward, and diagonally.

```
A W Y I S N O W W
W L J W O N S S S
S O S N O W N M
N S N T C O O M M
O N V S W C Y A
W O R N H P F Z
Z W O M L I T I
R T W O N S Y P
M M C Z P S E Z
```

© Dr. Seuss Enterprises, L.P.

The Cat in the Hat and his friends can't wait to play in the snow!

Nick, Sally, and the Fish make a snowman.

Circle the snowman that doesn't look like the others.

1.

2.

3.

4.

5.

6.

Ralph shows everyone his fancy moves on the ice!
He loves spinning around.

Draw yourself in Freeze-Your-Knees Snowland.

Thing One and Thing Two love swooshing down the hill!

Thing One and Thing Two love icicles.

Ralph and his parents wear harnesses for an important job.

Connect the dots to see what Ralph and his parents will pull for Santa on Christmas Eve.

It's time to get Nick and Sally back to their own
families for Christmas.

The Thinga-ma-jigger takes off for Nick and Sally's neighborhood.

The weather may make the ride home a little bumpy.
Can you find a safe path for the Cat?

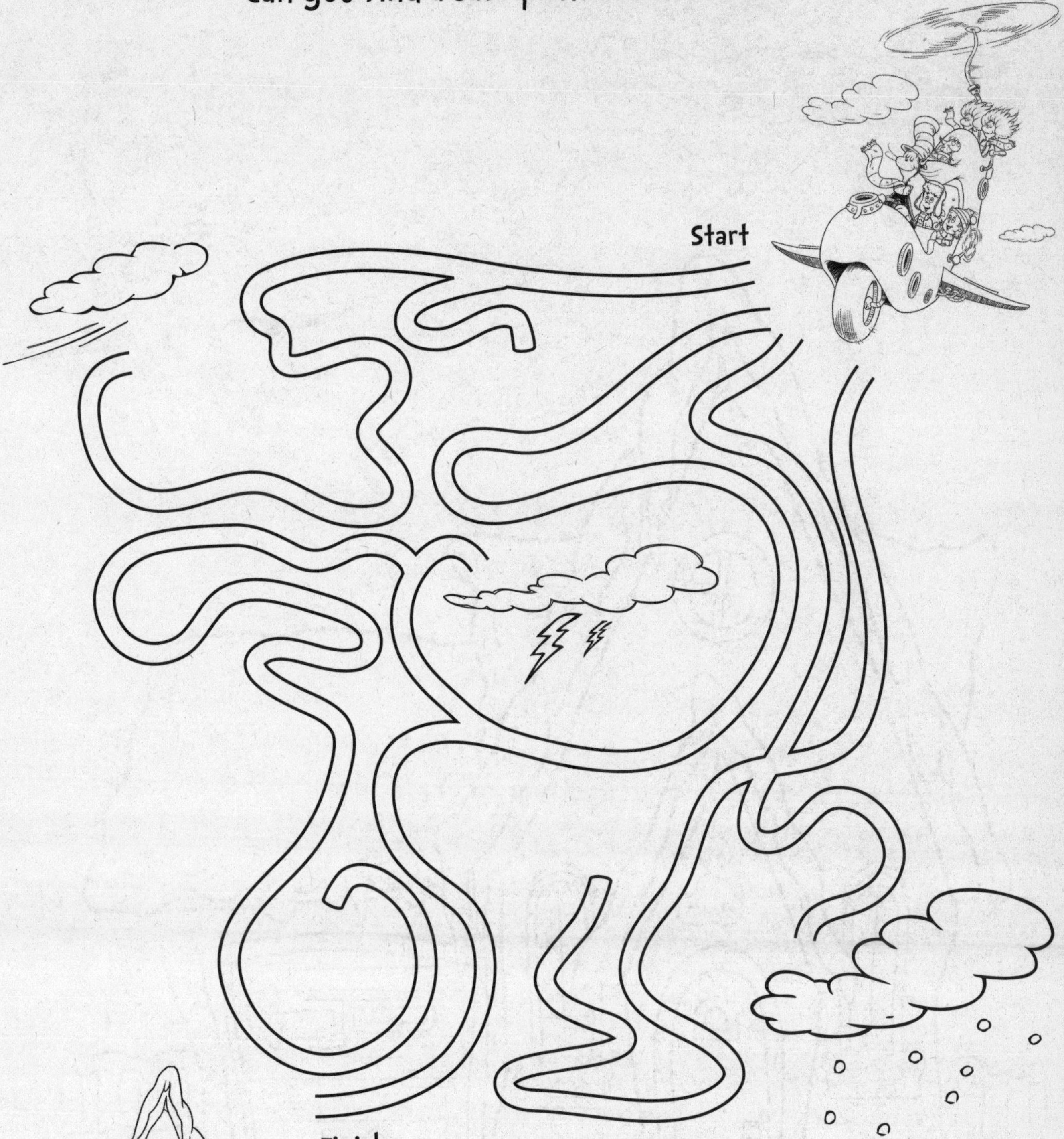

Start

Finish

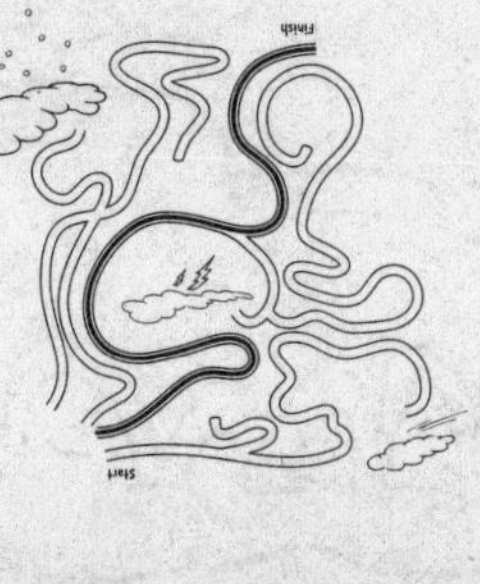

Nick and Sally are excited to be back home.

The Cat in the Hat hugs Nick and Sally goodbye and wishes them a merry Christmas.

Sally and Nick ask the Cat if he'd like to spend Christmas Eve with them.

Thing One and Thing Two put the finishing touches on the tree.

Thing One and Thing Two help Sally and Nick hang their stockings above the fireplace.

Sally and Nick put presents under the tree.

The Cat and his friends curl up on the couch so he can read
a Christmas story.

Sally and Nick fall fast asleep.
The Cat covers them with a blanket and quietly heads home.

Use the special code to reveal the secret holiday message.

"HO! HO! HO!"

MERRY CAT-MAS!